LOADING

VIRUS

CHRIS BRADFORD

With illustrations by
ANDERS FRANG

Barrington Stoke

**For more information on Chris and his books
visit: www.chrisbradford.co.uk**

First published in 2018 in Great Britain by
Barrington Stoke Ltd
18 Walker Street, Edinburgh, EH3 7LP

www.barringtonstoke.co.uk

Text © 2018 Chris Bradford
Illustrations © 2018 Anders Frang

A CIP catalogue record for this book is available
from the British Library upon request

ISBN: 978-1-78112-707-0

Printed in China by Leo

CONTENTS

Virtual Kombat is the most realistic fighting game ever. Choose your avatar and enter the VK battle arenas — where every enemy has a mind of its own. Feel the thrill ... *and* the pain of every fight!

THE ULTIMATE PRIZE!

Win the VK Crown and get ten million credits and your name in the Warrior Hall of Fame!

Are You An Elite Gamer?

KOMBAT

SO REAL IT HURTS

Watch out for the VK Selector Truck in *your* zone.

Jump into a PlayPod, play the game and prove your skills to win your place at Vince Power's Home for Elite Gamers!

WATCH VK LIVE

THE NO. 1 ENTERTAINMENT SHOW ON THE PLANET!

GAMER

UPDATE v1.1

This update provides key data for new and returning gamers:

- In the year 2030, a killer virus wiped out millions of adults and left a generation of orphans on the streets.

- Law and order collapsed and the military took over.

- Travel was restricted and curfews implemented.

- Adult survivors stayed indoors and escaped into a life on the internet.

- Virtual Kombat was invented by businessman Vince Power and became an instant hit when it went live in August 2031.

- VK was credited with cutting violent crime and restoring law and order in mega-cities around the world.

- Vince Power became a multi-billionaire and set up his City Orphans' Home for Elite Gamers in 2032.

- The VK Selector Truck began testing thousands of children and choosing Elite Gamers – saving them from starvation on the streets.

- Scott was one of the lucky kids chosen and trained as an Elite Gamer.

- But when his friend Kate died in the battle arena, Scott found out VK was *more* than just a game.

- Scott's discovery meant he was targeted for termination – his only choice was to go on the run ...

For a full update ... read GAMER, #1 in the Virtual Kombat series.

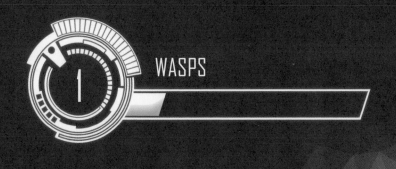

I sprint down the neon-lit street. My shoes pound on the cracked tarmac as hard as my heart beats. Running for my life, I splash in puddles of acid rain. But I don't care since I'm already soaked from jumping into the river to escape Vince Power.

The *buzz* of a Wasp chases me. The attack drone – a yellow and black machine of rotors and weapons – is a relentless hunter.

I bolt down an alley to my left. A bag of garbage almost trips me up. But I keep going. I ignore the stares of two street kids who are under a plastic sheet, sheltering from the rain.

The Wasp zooms past them too. Its Stinger is trained on just one target.

Me – Scott.

"*Stop or be stung!*" The Wasp's metallic voice echoes off the alley walls around me.

I glance back, feeling panicked. The Wasp's Stinger is locked and loaded, its red camera eye focused on me. I exit the alley into a street clogged with traffic and leap over the bonnet of an Auto-Taxi. The man inside glares at me, then spots the Wasp and dives behind his seat.

The Wasp fires its Stinger. I duck down. The electro-dart zips past my ear and hits a 3D Street Screen behind me. Sparks flare out of the screen like lightning bolts and the huge display explodes. The flash is blinding and cuts short an advert for Virtual Kombat: "SO REAL IT HURTS. THE ULTIM—"

I cover my head as glass rains down like razor-sharp hail. Then I dash into the alley opposite. I turn left. Then right. But the *whirr* of the Wasp's rotors is closing in on me.

I have to find somewhere to hide. And fast. It was pure luck that I wasn't hit by the first Stinger. Wasps *never* normally miss. Next time I might not be so lucky.

But my luck runs out sooner than I expect. I turn a corner and meet a dead end. A crumbling brick wall faces me and it's too high to climb. There are buildings on both sides but their doors are locked and the windows barred. My only way out is a metal fire escape that clings to one building like a rusty dead spider. I jump for the lower rung of the ladder ... but it's beyond my reach.

I think of my VK avatar's super strength and wish I had it in the real world!

The Wasp turns the corner and hovers in front of me.

"*Surrender!*" the drone orders, and targets its Stinger on my chest.

I can't let myself be caught. People need to know the truth about VK. It's down to me and me alone. I'm the only hope for those Elite Gamers still trapped in the game.

I pick up a loose brick from the ground and hurl it at the Wasp. The drone dodges it, so I throw another brick. This time it sails high and the Wasp doesn't even bother to move. I swear I can almost hear the Wasp's operator laughing at my poor aim. But I'm determined to have the last laugh!

I launch a third brick. This one hits the metal fire escape and knocks the ladder's catch.

The ladder drops down and smashes into the Wasp. It spirals to the ground, its *buzz* dies and its red camera eye blinks out.

"Swatted!" I shout, and punch the air in victory.

But the grin falls from my face as three more Wasps swarm into the alley.

2 ONLY A GAME

I scramble up the fire escape and onto the roof where I'm greeted by more 3D Street Screens. They glow like full moons in the city's choking grey smog. The perfect suntanned face of Vince Power looms out from every screen, his silver-white hair glinting like snow.

"LIVE! FIGHT! KILL!" Vince declares as Virtual Kombat, the number one video game on the planet, is introduced with a fanfare of horns and drums. The credits roll: *Where every enemy has a mind of its own* ... and a match between Goliath and the Reaper is replayed in such high definition that the avatars move, breathe and bleed as if they're alive.

Goliath swings a
spiked iron club at
his opponent's head.
The Reaper, in his
ash-coloured gown,
turns to smoke and the club misses.
Then the Reaper reappears and cuts
down with his long curved blade, slicing
Goliath completely in half. "KILLING
STRIKE!" the commentator shouts ...

Vince Power's face returns to the
screens as he says, "In the virtual world
of VK, there are no limits to what you
can do." He flashes a perfect white smile
and adds, "After all ... it's only a game!"

But I know it *isn't* only a game. To play is
to die.

I've seen the brains of young players
burned out and destroyed. Each VK avatar
in the game is powered by a homeless kid
recruited from the streets by the VK Selector

Truck. Just like I was. It means that when a gamer kills an avatar in the virtual arena, that kid dies in the real world too. The PlayPods are simply too powerful for our young minds. So we blow like a fuse.

I think of my friend Kate dying in my arms and my heart burns with grief and rage. She was killed in the game by my sworn enemy, Shark. I can still remember how her eyes sparked blue then faded like a wilting flower, and I vow to save the rest of the Elite Gamers. I vow to bring Vince Power to justice. Somehow I must stop VK. End the game.

But I am the only person in the outside world who knows Vince's dark secret – that kids burn out in VK. That is the reason Vince wants me ... alive or dead!

The *buzz* of Wasps suddenly grows louder. I dart behind a screen and find a door into the building. But when I yank on the handle, the door is stuck. A Wasp zooms in to attack me. Gritting my teeth, I pull with all my strength. The door hinges squeal in protest but a narrow gap appears between the door and frame. I hear the *zing* of a Stinger and throw myself inside. The Stinger sparks off the metal frame. I heave the door shut and race down the stairs but I have to stop halfway to catch my breath.

The walls are covered in graffiti and the stairwell stinks of urine and rubbish. Strip lights flicker in the ceiling overhead. The hallway on this level is deserted but that's no surprise. Few people leave their homes now. Fear of the killer virus of 2030 keeps them inside. They'd rather be plugged into the virtual world of the net, safe from harm.

With all the doors locked, I know I can't hide here for long. The Wasps will just patrol the building and wait for Vince's Analysts to turn up and capture me. So I descend to the ground floor and head for the rear fire exit. Kicking it open, I dash out into an old basketball court, its hoops rusted and bent. No games are played here. No one even owns a basketball any more. But the court isn't empty ...

"Look what the cat's dragged in!" sneers a voice I recognise.

3

I spin round to see a lanky boy with a slick of black hair and a busted nose. Several other street kids are standing behind him.

"Stick?" I gasp. He's taller than I remember. The last time I saw him, he and Shark were chasing me across the rooftops.

Stick takes in my wet VK kombat suit, with *SCOTT* stitched in white across the black fabric. "You look like a drowned rat!" he laughs.

"I jumped off a building into the river," I explain.

Stick snorts as if he doesn't believe me. "I thought you'd be dead by now. Shark vowed to blaze you. He followed the VK Selector Truck for weeks until he won a place in Vince Power's Orphans' Home."

"It's no home," I reply. "It's a slaughterhouse. Vince uses the kids there as cattle for his VK game. The PlayPods burn out our brains! But I managed to escape."

"What a load of bull, Scott!" Stick says with a cold laugh. "I bet you were thrown out for not being good enough. But ... your loss is my gain."

Stick clicks his fingers and his gang surround me. Some are carrying steel pipes, others twirl bike chains as weapons.

"Wait!" I cry, holding up my hands. I realise if I'm going to have any chance of defeating Vince Power, I'll need help – even from my enemies. "Didn't you hear me? Virtual Kombat is *killing* people."

Stick looks at me as if I'm stupid. "*Doh!* That's the whole point of the game."

"No, for real!" I tell Stick. "You *have* to believe me." As his gang moves in, I rack my brains for a way to convince Stick of what I'm saying ... "Shark is in danger too."

Stick hesitates, frowns and then puffs out his bony chest. "Who cares? *I'm* gang leader now."

He pulls a Blazer from his pocket and flicks on the red pulsing blade. All my hopes of getting Stick to help fade. He points the Blazer's tip at me. "*You*, Scott, have a debt to pay for my friend Juice's death."

I back away. "I didn't kill him. He fell!"

"He fell because of you!" Stick moves to blaze me but at that moment the high-pitched *whirr* of Wasps enters the basketball court. For a second, the gang freeze and stare with horror at the yellow and black drones. Then they scatter in all directions, like startled cats.

A Wasp has me in its sights and fires its Stinger just as Stick turns to flee.

"Watch out!" I shout at Stick, but the warning comes too late. He runs straight into the Stinger's path and it strikes him in the chest. He slumps to the ground and thrashes wildly as he's paralysed by the electro-dart.

The three Wasps now close in on me. I dive into the nearest alley, praying I don't end up like Stick. But in my rush I don't look where I am going. I fall into an open grate and crash-land in a sewer tunnel. The Wasps buzz in a circle above me as I lie in the tunnel, winded and defenceless.

This time there is no escape.

The three Wasps direct their Stingers at me.
I tense my muscles, bracing myself for the
searing pain ... but it doesn't come. The Wasps
suddenly stop whirring, their red camera eyes
blink out and they drop to the tunnel floor like
dead flies. I stare at the machines, confused.

Then a girl with short dark hair and a
pale face steps from the shadows of the sewer.
There's a stripe of black make-up across her
cat-like eyes and she's holding a device that
looks like a small gun without a barrel.

"EMP," the girl explains, and taps one of the
Wasps with her boot. She sees my puzzled face.

"It stands for Electro-Magnetic Pulse weapon. The EMP shorts out the Wasps' circuits. For a while, at least."

I get to my feet and dust myself off. "Well, thanks for saving me."

She shoots me a look. "I wasn't saving *you*. I was worried they'd see *me*!" She bends down and picks up a Wasp. "Now, help me get these out of the tunnel before they re-boot."

She throws the drone up into the alley, then climbs out herself. I grab the other two Wasps and toss them to her. Then I join the girl on street level. As she pushes the grate of the sewer back into place, I can't help but ask, "What were you doing down there?"

One of the Wasps starts to buzz back to life.

"I'd get out of here if I were you," the girl says, striding away down the alley.

I race after her. "Who are you? What's your name?"

She walks faster.

"Where are you going in such a rush?" I demand.

The girl flips up the hood of her jacket and continues to ignore me. I jog to keep up as she turns the corner and heads down a back street. "Why would the Wasps be interested in *you* anyway?" I ask her.

"Zap off!" she snaps, and swings into an unlit alleyway.

For a moment, I think of letting her go. But even if she's rude, she's just the sort of person who needs to know about VK. I have to convince her of VK's deadly truth. And if I can't persuade her, I need her EMP gun at the very least. The Wasps won't ever stop hunting me but with that device I can stop them. So I chase after her and grab her arm. "Where did you get that weapon?"

The girl shakes herself free and glares at me. "You ask a lot of questions, Wasp Boy!"

"That's because I need a lot of answers," I reply. "Listen, I'm in big trouble and I *really* need one of those EMP weapons."

She puts her hands on her hips. "Why?"

We hold each other's stares. She's acting strange and secretive but I have no choice but to trust her. "Because I'm on the run from Vince Power," I explain. "I was an Elite Gamer for him in VK. But I found out that he's—"

"You're a Gamer?" she interrupts. I nod. She narrows her jet-black eyes. "I don't believe you. No one escapes the game."

"Well, I did."

"*Really?*" She takes a step closer, studying my face and VK kombat suit. Then I feel two metal prongs on my stomach and a jolt of electricity blazes into my system. My body locks up. The pain overcomes me and I black out …

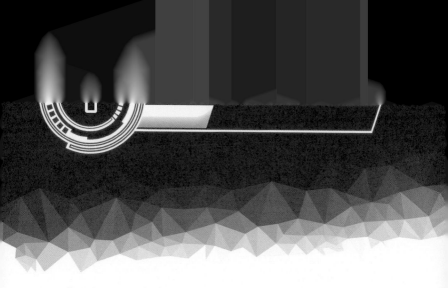

I wake in a small white room without windows. My hands and feet are tied to a hospital bed. I'm alone. A prisoner. I curse to myself. The girl must have turned me in! Handed me over to Vince Power in exchange for a reward. I should *never* have trusted her.

I sit up and tug at my bonds but the ties just close around my wrists and ankles. The more I struggle, the tighter they become.

Relax, I tell myself. My father – before he died of the virus – was a soldier in the SAS. He taught me how to get out of wrist ties. First, it's important to loosen your muscles.

As soon as I do this and stop pulling, the ties seem to release. In fact, the more I relax, the easier it is to slip free. In seconds, my hands are out and I can undo my ankle ties and jump off the bed.

But I'm still trapped in the room. There doesn't seem to be a door. I run my fingers along the gleaming white walls. They're as smooth as glass and it takes me three goes around the room before I feel the faint outline of a door frame. But there's no handle or keypad to open it.

I slump down on the bed. With no way out, I'm still a prisoner. I can only wait for someone to appear. Defeated, I flop back on the thin mattress. That's when I feel cool air on my face and see the ventilation panel in the ceiling.

Standing on the bed, I reach up and pull the panel free. The ventilation shaft is dark and narrow but I'm just slim enough to fit. Lifting myself up, I squeeze into the duct and crawl along. Ahead I can see a glimmer of light. I come to another panel, punch it out and drop to the floor.

I land in a corridor lined with doors, each numbered and locked by a digital keypad. There's no one around and this makes me nervous as I creep along, corridor after corridor. They all look the same: white, blank and empty. I feel like a lab rat in a maze.

Then, as I turn a corner, I come across a ventilation panel lying on the floor. The one I punched out.

I've been going round in circles!

I keep going, searching for a route out. But I end up at the panel again. My third attempt brings me back to the exact same spot. Frustrated, I kick the panel. *The building is a labyrinth!*

I stare in fury at the rows of locked doors. *How am I ever going to escape?*

Then I notice the numbers on the doors. On my right I count off: 1 ... 4 ... 6 ...

On my left I read: 2 ... 3 ... 5 ...

Their order seems strange. The odd and even numbers mixed up. I walk to the first junction of the next corridor. 7 ... 11 ... 13 ... go one way and 8 ... 9 ... 10 ... the other way.

It makes no sense at all. There seems to be no logic to them. Then I recall a maths lesson from my distant past, before the virus turned the whole world upside down. There was a set of random numbers we studied. *What were they called?*

Prime numbers, that's it! Numbers that are only divisible by themselves and 1.

And 2, 3, 5, 7, 11 and 13 are all prime numbers.

I follow the trail, feeling excited by my discovery. My brain almost overloads as I try to work out each prime number in order: 13 ... 17 ... 19 ... 23 ... 29 ...

I arrive at a door with no number. Just a keypad. My finger trembles as I punch in the next prime number: 31. The lock clicks and the door slides open. Beyond it is a paved courtyard. My heart lifts as I step towards freedom. Then my foot trips a laser sensor, an alarm blares out and my stomach sinks.

Three security guards rush into the courtyard. I turn to flee but find the door has locked shut behind me. The courtyard is enclosed, with the building rising up to the sky on all sides. Then I spot a green EXIT sign beyond the three guards.

My only way out is past them.

The first guard comes thundering at me with his baton raised. I block his strike to my head and punch him hard in the stomach. He doubles over and I elbow him in the temple. The man goes down.

The second guard charges in. I jump to one side and give him a roundhouse-kick to the gut. But this guard is stronger. He takes the blow, then lashes out with a 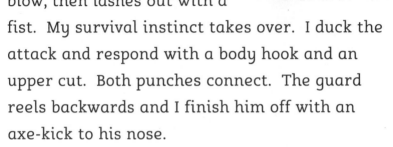 fist. My survival instinct takes over. I duck the attack and respond with a body hook and an upper cut. Both punches connect. The guard reels backwards and I finish him off with an axe-kick to his nose.

My father, a black belt in *tae kwon do*, taught me how to fight. But even I'm surprised at my skills right now. I feel as powerful as my VK avatar.

The last guard is big ... and far more wary. He waits for me to approach him.

Feeling confident, I launch a side-kick at him then a back-kick. But the guard swats them off and counters with a powerful front-kick that sends me flying across the courtyard. I scramble back to my feet, pain rippling through my chest. The guard comes at me again. We swap blows and he catches me on the jaw with a hook punch. Stars burst before my eyes and I have to retreat.

"Is that all you've got, pipsqueak?" the guard grunts.

This just makes me angry, so I run at him and leap into the air. Twisting, I let loose a spinning hook-kick. The guard is taken by surprise as my heel smashes into his head. He collapses like a felled tree.

I'm almost as stunned as the guard by my incredible kick. But I don't get time to celebrate. A door behind me slides open and more security guards spill into the courtyard. I dash for the green EXIT sign and enter a stairwell. I race up several levels but hear feet pounding after me. At the top of the stairs I come to another door and burst out onto the building's flat roof.

I peer over the edge and see the street twenty storeys below. I begin to feel desperate as I look around for another way down. There's a building opposite this one, its roof a bit lower. But the gap looks too wide for even me to jump. I'd have to clear almost ten metres!

A unit of guards fan out around me with their batons raised to attack. I turn to face them. But there's no way I can defeat them all. I'm left with no choice – do or die. So I take a running leap off the roof for the other building. My legs pedal wildly and my arms wheel in an effort to cross the gap. The roof opposite rushes towards me but I'm falling too fast. Horror strikes me as I realise I'm *not* going to make it ...

My body is throbbing with pain. My limbs feel like cracked glass. I can taste blood in my mouth ...

But I'm not dead. In fact, I don't think I've broken a single bone.

Opening my eyes, I see three kids looking down at me. One of them is the girl with the black stripe of make-up from the sewer. The girl who electro-stunned me.

"He's an Elite Gamer all right!" a small boy cries. He's chubby, with glasses and a mop of sandy hair. "We are so made. Nothing can stop us now, not even the Reaper—"

"Shut it, Spam!" the girl snaps. "We don't know anything about this boy. Except the fact he wants to die."

"Don't be so hard on him," a stocky lad says. His faded T-shirt has a yellow Pac-Man on the front, stretched tight by the lad's bulging muscles. "No one has ever got *that* far in the Trial, not even you, Java."

The girl, who must be Java, shoots the lad a sharp look. "He failed. He *died*. He's no good to us."

There's a muffled cough and everyone turns to a slim dark girl with a fringe of brown hair covering her eyes. She is sitting at the controls of an Analyst console in the centre of the room. "You should take a look at his synapse readings," she suggests in a low voice.

As we all turn to the console screen, I realise I'm lying in a makeshift PlayPod. Not as sleek as Vince Power's units, it's more functional, like a speeder bike with its engine showing. There are three more PlayPods hooked into the console but these are empty. The room is cluttered with circuit boards, spare parts and scrap metal. The place looks like a motor repair shop. I take off my hoody headset and the throbbing in my bones fades. Only then does it dawn on me that my imprisonment and escape weren't real. My fall from the rooftop was just an illusion. My pain no more than a computer effect.

I'd been plugged into a virtual arena!

On the console screen is a replay of my fight with the guards.

"His reaction time is less than fifty milliseconds," the console girl says as she studies the data. "That's a full ten milliseconds faster than even Pac-Man here." She nods at the stocky lad, then looks back at me and adds, "Our new friend solved the puzzle of the wrist ties in under a minute – he knew that struggling just made them tighter. He found the *one* way out of the White Room. *And* he escaped the maze by working out the prime-number trail."

A grin spreads across my face. They were all tests and I passed! *But for what?*

"Don't give him a big head, Cookie," Java warns. "Don't forget he tripped the sensor."

Cookie shrugs and turns away from the console. "I programmed the Trial to do that whatever happens – so a gamer's combat skills can be tested."

"Yeah, and he wasted those guards!" Spam says. He pumps a fist as we watch my avatar on screen take down the biggest guard. "Just look at that flying spinning hook-kick!"

"That was super cool," Pac-Man agrees. He winks at me. "Gotta teach me that move, Scott."

"Errr … sure," I reply. "But I don't understand what's g—"

"Is no one listening to me?" Java says. "The guy has a death wish. He jumped off the roof! We can't rely on him."

"*Excuse me!*" I interrupt. "What are you all talking about?" But they just keep on arguing.

"He took a calculated risk," Cookie says. She raises an eyebrow. "Have any of you ever attempted the leap?"

Java crosses her arms and scowls. "No, because it's impossible!"

"Nothing is impossible in VK," a voice as smooth as silk says from behind me.

I jump out of my PlayPod, shocked. Sitting in the shadows is a silver-haired man with a pearly white smile ... Vince Power.

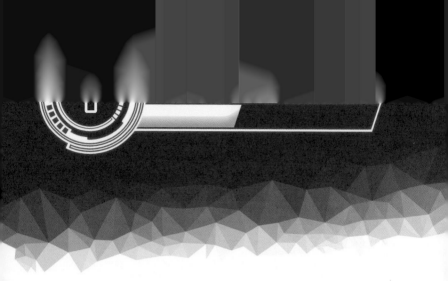

I grab a metal pipe from the floor and swing it wildly at Vince and the others to keep them away.

"Put the weapon down, Scott," Vince orders.

I tighten my grip on the pipe. "I'm not playing any more of your games, Vince."

The man snorts a hollow laugh. "*Vince?* I'm not Vince."

My eyes narrow. "Then who are you?"

"His brother. His twin, actually."

"*Brother?*" I feel my legs go weak with a mix of shock and exhaustion.

"My name is Pentium," the man says. He glides forward in a motorised wheelchair. "And by your reaction to me, you must hate Vince almost as much as I do."

In the light, Pentium's face is pale and wrinkled. He may look like Vince but he doesn't have his brother's tanned, perfect skin. I lower the metal pipe. Pentium waves towards the door and says, "Come, let's have some food. Then I'll explain."

I follow Pentium and the others along a tunnel into a dim foyer. There's a row of dead ticket machines and a set of silent and still escalators leading down into darkness.

"Where are we?" I ask.

"An old subway station," Spam replies cheerfully. "Makes a good place to hide. No

Wasp will ever find us. We're
right under—" But Spam stops as
Java shoots him a hard stare.

We enter an area marked "Staff Only".
There's a small canteen with an auto-meal
vending machine. I order chicken noodles,
then take a seat with the others at a table. My
hunger is stronger than my curiosity, so I gulp
down the food first. Then I ask, "So who are
you people?"

"The VKR – Virtual Kombat Rebellion," Spam
says proudly.

I frown. "VKR? Never heard of you."

"Good," Java replies in a tone as cold as ice.
"And we want to keep it that way."

I give her a suspicious look. "Why? What
are you up to?"

"First, let me give you a bit of background, Scott," Pentium says, and moves himself to the head of the table. "The world might believe that Vince Power invented Virtual Kombat, but *I* was the real programmer."

I blink with shock. Every advert and piece of news coverage gives the impression that Vince alone created VK.

"I had the brains and IT skills," Pentium continues. "My brother had the creativity and the flair to sell the idea to the world. We made a good team and Virtual Kombat was a positive thing when it began. A much-needed way to escape the horrors of the real world."

Pentium takes a sip from his vita-shake, his hands trembling with the effort of lifting the cup.

"That was until Vince took the game one step too far," Pentium goes on. "He noticed that as VK became more violent, more players joined and we made more money. Even when we discovered the hoodies could cause Burn Out in kids, Vince didn't stop the game. In fact, he *sold* the idea to the highest bidders! 'Kill for Real' was his slogan. Murder without punishment."

"*So you know too?*" I gasp. "That he's killing innocent kids?"

With grave faces, Pentium and the others nod their heads.

"That's when I decided to pull the plug on VK," Pentium reveals. "Vince didn't agree, of course. We were making too much money. We had too much power by then. So he plugged *me* into the game. He even offered prize money to the gamer who killed my avatar! Vince sabotaged my hoody and disabled my ESCAPE button to make sure I wouldn't survive. But he didn't know that I'd programmed back doors into the game."

I can't help but smile when I hear this. "Yeah, I know," I say. "I used one to escape VK!"

"Well, I'm glad you got out unhurt," Pentium replies. "I was close to death – just had 2% on my life-bar when I reached the door. It was a miracle I hadn't burned out. But I *was* left in a coma for months, and when I awoke, discovered I was paralysed from the waist down." Pentium pats his wheelchair and gives a heavy sigh. "Vince put me in a secure hospital. He never visits, so believes I'm still there."

I look at Pentium, then round at the others in his team. Relief and hope fill me. Relief that I'm not the only one to know VK's dark secret. And hope that I've found the help I was looking for. "So what's VKR's purpose?"

A sly grin spreads across Pentium's wrinkled face. "To take VK offline. For good. The question is ... will *you* join us in our fight?"

I don't need asking twice. I smile and nod. "Your plan is my plan."

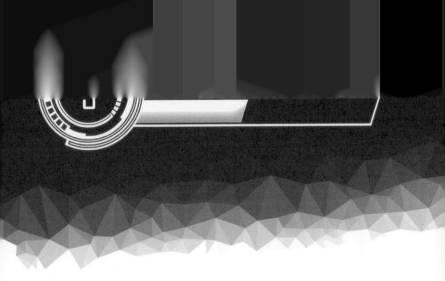

Yawning, I enter the console room with Spam the next morning. After dinner last night, I'd been shown to a dorm – a row of bunk beds in an old storage room. I'd crashed out, so tired I didn't even take my shoes off!

Looking around, I see that Cookie is programming the console, Pac-Man is preparing the PlayPods and Java is whispering with Pentium in the corner. There's a total of five people in the room.

"Is this *all* of the VKR?" I ask.

"Well ... there were others," Spam admits. He adjusts his glasses and gives me an uneasy smile. "But the game has taken its toll."

When Pentium asked me to join the Virtual Kombat Rebellion, I jumped at the chance. But now I'm not so sure that I made the right decision. The task of bringing down VK seems impossible with so few of us.

"*Are you sure about him?*" Java hisses to Pentium.

"We need an Elite Gamer who takes risks," Pentium replies.

"Yeah, but not at *our* risk!" Java argues.

"You're the one who brought him in."

"I made a mistake," she counters.

"Did y—" Pentium starts, but then sees me and smiles. "Ah, Scott!"

Java stalks off and joins the others by the PlayPods.

"What's her problem?" I ask Pentium.

He sighs and explains, "Java's protective of her team. She lost her sister to VK."

"Oh … I'm sorry." After my own loss, I understand how upset and angry Java might feel.

"She knows one mistake could end in death," Pentium goes on. "But we need to keep pushing on if we're to succeed with our plan."

"So what is this plan?" I ask.

Pentium steers his wheelchair over to the console. "Cookie's the best one to bring you up to speed."

Cookie saves Pac-Man's Mods to his avatar, then swivels round in the control chair. "In theory, it's pretty straightforward," she says. "We use this console to remotely hack into the VK game and plug you and the team into the virtual arena. Then your task is to install a virus to destroy VK."

I frown. "If you can hack into the game, why not just implant the virus remotely? Why do you need to risk our lives in VK?"

"The program doesn't work like that," Cookie explains. "VK firewalls would destroy the virus before it got anywhere near the core programming. But if it's programmed from within the game itself, the virus acts like a cancer cell in a body. It multiplies and spreads. Nothing can stop it."

"So where do we have to install this virus?" I ask.

"In the Crown."

"I know where the Crown is!" I cry. "I saw it in the Sky Citadel."

Cookie shakes her head. "That's not the *real* VK Crown. That's a fake – a decoy. The Crown is the highest stage of VK – the Last Level. Reach that and you control the game."

"Once we get to that level," says Java, turning to us from her PlayPod, "there's a virtual terminal – the nexus of the game – into which we input the virus. Then BOOM ..." A dark gleam enters Java's eyes and she spreads her fingers to mimic an explosion. "It's all over."

"Sounds simple," I say.

"Not really," Pac-Man grunts, and climbs into his PlayPod. "We're still three levels away. And we have to get past the Reaper first."

"Yeah," Spam says, and goes pale as he straps himself into his own seat. "The

Reaper is unbeatable. We've almost died five times already!"

"Can't we skip a level?" I ask. "Avoid the Reaper?" I turn to Pentium. "You must know some cheats or a shortcut?"

Pentium shakes his head. "I may have programmed VK myself, but Vince's Analysts then changed many elements in the game to make it more demanding *and* profitable. Also, I had to bury the virtual terminal deep within VK so that my brother wouldn't notice it. I'm afraid … the only way is to play."

Java jumps into her PlayPod. "Well, what are you waiting for, Wasp Boy?"

I hesitate. "Won't Vince's Analysts know we've hacked into the game?"

Cookie chews her lower lip. "They shouldn't. We're using the avatars of dead gamers. And it's just four players among millions, so we should slip under their radar. Well, we have done so far."

Ignoring my nerves, I clamber into the spare PlayPod and strap myself in.

Cookie makes a final systems check, then says, "Same rules apply as before. Same risk of Burn Out. You die in the game, you die in real life. Since we're hacking in, there's no ESCAPE button. But Pentium's back doors are still there – they're your *only* way out."

"Great," I reply with a strained smile. "Anything else I should know?"

As the silver helmet of the hoody slides down over my face, Cookie adds, "Yeah, it's a wireless connection. If the connection fails, you'll be trapped inside the game for ever."

"*What?*" I cry. But it's too late. I'm plugged into VK.

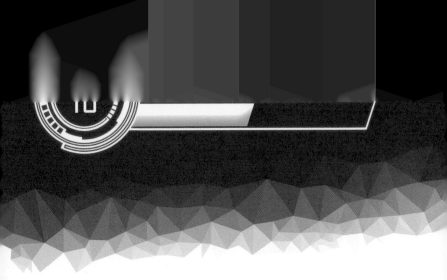

A mountain rises up before me, so high I can't even see its peak. A waterfall pours down the side into a lake. At the mountain's base is a cave, its entrance as jagged as a monster's mouth. Once again I am stunned by the scale and detail of VK's virtual world.

An Amazonian warrior is standing beside me. "The next level is inside that cave," she says. She's dressed in leather armour and carries a silver sword. A black stripe is painted across her eyes. It's Java.

I look down. My avatar is a kickboxer – black sneakers, red slacks and a white vest over toned muscles.

"If it all goes wrong, head to that waterfall," a cowboy drawls. He's wearing a suede jacket and has two six-shooters on his hip. Pac-Man's rugged features are scanned onto the cowboy's face. "It's a back door," he explains.

I nod at Pac-Man as Spam bumps into me.

"I can't see a thing in this!" Spam complains, and snaps up the visor of his helmet. His avatar is a space trooper armed with a laser rifle.

"You *chose* that suit," Java snorts as she strides off towards the cave.

"Because it had the most armour protection!" Spam replies. He lumbers after her.

I follow behind with Pac-Man. The tunnel is as dark as night. Spam uses his head torch to light the way. The rock walls gleam like black blood and the temperature drops to freezing.

Pac-Man draws his pistols. "Keep sharp! The Reaper's ghosts are near."

Looking at Pac-Man's guns, Spam's rifle and Java's sword, I now wish I had a weapon. I raise my fists as the tunnel opens out into a huge cavern. The vile stink of sulphur rises from a pool of red-hot lava.

All of a sudden, Spam starts firing his rifle as black ghosts swoop down. Laser shots blast the walls and send chunks of rock flying. Java swings her sword, slicing one ghost in half and turning it to ash. Pac-Man guns down three more. I duck as a ghost tries to dive into me.

Then I throw a punch at another. My fist turns ice cold as the ghost swallows my entire arm. My avatar's life-bar drops ... 98% ... 95% ... 90% ...

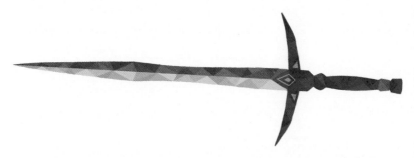

"Don't touch them!" Java cries. She cuts the ghost on my arm to ash.

"How am I meant to kill them then?" I ask as I shake the numbness from my arm.

"You can't," Java says. "That's our job. You deal with *him*."

I turn to see the Reaper rising from the lava pool. He floats towards me in a grey gown, his skeletal hands holding a long curved scythe. With vicious speed, he swipes with his blade. I leap over the razor-sharp steel and kick him in the chest. The gown crumples but there's nothing there for me to hit and the Reaper is left unharmed. The scythe swipes again and I almost lose my head. I kick, punch and strike with all my skill and strength. But it's as if I'm fighting against thin air.

With all the ghosts destroyed, the others join me to battle the Reaper. But their bullets and laser shots just pass through him. And when Java cuts at the Reaper with her sword, he turns to smoke.

"He can't be killed!" I shout.

"*We know*," Java replies as her eyes dart around for the Reaper. "We hoped an Elite Gamer like you could defeat him. But I see we were wrong!"

Suddenly the Reaper appears next to Spam. His scythe slashes across the space trooper's armoured chest. Spam falls to the ground and the Reaper goes for a killing strike.

"NO!" I cry as the tip of the Reaper's blade strikes at Spam's heart.

I focus on the scythe. Watch the blade come down. See Spam scream in terror ...

As I concentrate on the Reaper's every move, his attack slows. I rush forward and kick the long handle of the scythe. It snaps in half. A shriek rings out and the Reaper vanishes. His gown flops to the floor, empty and smoking.

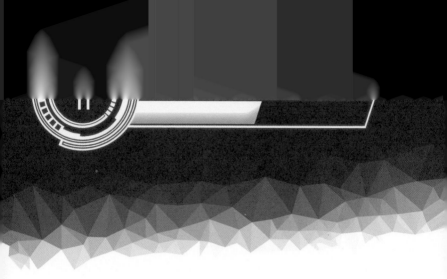

"How did you do *that?*" Spam gasps. He lies on the floor beside the Reaper's gown, with blood seeping from his chest.

"Trigger Time," I reply. The team look at me, confused. "If you focus hard enough, you can slow down virtual time," I explain. "Your brain has to work faster than the game can download into your head. But it only ever lasts a few seconds."

"That explains your reaction speed," Java says. "But how did Trigger Time kill the Reaper?" She helps Spam to his feet and gives him a health pack. His life-bar returns to 100%.

Cookie's voice speaks in our heads – via her console comms link. *"The scythe must have been the Reaper's source of power."*

Spam rolls his eyes. "And to think we've been trying to kill *him*, when all along it was his weapon!"

"Great work, Scott!" Pac-Man says, and slaps me on the back.

I grin. "Thanks."

"Come on!" Java orders. She seems less impressed. "We need to find the portal to the next level."

We search the cavern and find the portal on the other side of the lava pool – a spinning whirlpool of stars and galaxies in the floor. I hold my breath as the four of us link hands and jump ...

⏸

In a blaze of light, we're transported to the edge of a Wild West town.

"*According to Pentium,*" Cookie says over the comms link, "*this level should be the Temple of the Ten Tigers.*"

Java frowns. "So where's the temple?"

"Must be another upgrade," Spam sighs.

"Keep an eye out for old markers then," says Pac-Man. He looks the part of the outlaw as we enter the town and stroll along a dusty street lined with wooden-slatted buildings. At its centre we come to a crossroads with an old stone well.

Cookie's voice comes online to tell us, "*The well is a back door.*"

"A marker!" Spam says. "At least we're on the right track."

"But which way do we head now?" I ask. To the north is a forest, to the south is a lake and to the west a desert. Each option looks no more promising than the next.

Java shrugs. "Your guess is as good as mine—"

A shout comes from inside a saloon bar. A second later, the swing doors of the bar fly open and a body is hurled out. It lands in the street, kicking up a cloud of dust. Three cowboys stride out of the saloon towards the groaning body. As the dust settles, I see the black outfit and mask of a ninja ... and a tuft of red hair poking out. I know who this is ...

"Ginger Ninja!" I cry. I thought my friend had been killed in VK. But here he is, alive and ... Well, alive for the moment. One of the cowboys is drawing his pistol at him.

I run to save Ginger Ninja and Java shouts, "He's not our mission, Scott."

But I ignore her as I kick the gun from the cowboy's hand, then back-fist him in the head. His Stetson hat goes flying and he falls to the ground. The other two cowboys reach for their guns. I knife-hand one in the neck and palm-strike the other in the face. Then finish them off with a double flying-kick.

Java gives me a slow clap. "Impressive, Scott. Now you've saved him, let's go!"

I help my friend up. "Are you OK, Ginger Ninja?"

He looks at me. His eyes narrow then widen when he recognises me. "Scott?"

I nod, pleased that the game hasn't taken away all of his memory. Last time I saw him, he tried to kill me.

"But which way *do* we go?" Spam asks Java, and turns a circle at the crossroads. "We don't know where the Temple of the Ten Tigers is!"

"I do," Ginger Ninja pipes up.

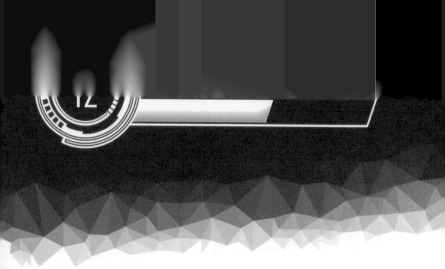

"That's karma for you," I tell Java as we trek north through a bamboo forest. "If I hadn't saved my friend here, we'd still be lost."

She gives me a sideways look. "We're not there yet."

"How much further?" I ask Ginger Ninja.

"Oh, not far," he replies, trotting alongside me. "So where have you been, Scott? You vanished from the arena."

"I escaped VK."

62

Ginger Ninja's eyebrows shoot up. "*How?*"

"I found a—"

"Are you *sure* this is the way?" Java interrupts me as the path disappears and the forest grows thicker.

Ginger Ninja nods. "The temple is hidden. Follow the white bamboo."

Among the green bamboo stems, there is a line of white stalks leading deeper into the forest. We follow the trail, passing a Shinto shrine with a stone gateway covered in moss.

Cookie's voice sounds in our heads: "*That's another back door.*"

"Good to know," Pac-Man replies out loud.

Ginger Ninja didn't hear Cookie and shoots Pac-Man an odd look. Leaning close to me, he whispers, "So how did you meet these crazy guys?"

"We're—"

"Seeking the Crown," Java cuts over me. "Like everyone else."

Ginger Ninja smiles. "Teamwork, eh?"

All of a sudden, the forest opens out onto a temple courtyard. Ten stone tigers on pedestals line a pathway that leads to a huge wooden building with a curved roof.

"I guess this is it then," Spam says.

Java scans the empty courtyard. "I don't like the look of this," she says, drawing her sword.

We creep towards the temple, passing between the tigers. I feel their eyes watching

me. *"They're made of stone,"* I tell myself as I
try to shrug off my unease.

Then an avatar in
a long black leather
jacket and dark shades
steps from the temple.

He grins to reveal a row of sharp-pointed teeth.
I gasp, shocked. It's my sworn enemy, Shark.

"At long last I've found you, Scott!" Shark
snarls, closing his fists. Two pulse-blades burst
from his knuckles, the laser knives crackling
with energy. A high-level Mod. He ignites two
pulse-blades from his fists and commands,
"Tigers awake!"

The stone statues come to life and leap
from their pedestals with their eyes blazing
and their fangs bared. Java cuts one down as it
pounces but another lands on her back and digs
its claws into her leather armour. Spam fires
his laser rifle, blasting chunks out of the other
beasts. Pac-Man wrestles a tiger to the ground,

too caught by surprise to draw his guns in time. Ginger Ninja is lost among the fighting.

Shark strides towards me, his pulse-blades glowing. "Blaze and burn time!"

He lashes out with an attack so fast I barely see it. The blade slices me across the arm. I cry out in pain as the smell of my burning flesh fills the air. My life-bar flashes 80% as I dodge his next attack and counter with a side-kick. But Shark easily evades it and blazes my thigh. I'm at 69% as I limp away, wondering how he can react so fast.

Then I remember ... *Trigger Time!*

As Shark thrusts his pulse-blade at me again, I focus my mind and break down his movements until the virtual world slows. The pulse-blade turns from a blur to a dagger of red light. Now I'm faster than him, for a few seconds at least, I manage to block his attack

and hit back with a devastating punch to his ribs. I hear the crack of bone—

Then Trigger Time comes to an end and VK zips back to normal speed. Shark's pulse-blade tears into me yet again. I'm forced back, each blaze reducing my life-bar ... 60% ... 53% ... 42% ...

I'm on the point of defeat when Pac-Man throws the tiger he's wrestling at my attacker. The beast claws at Shark's leather jacket, ripping it to shreds.

"Let's go! To the back door!" Pac-Man orders, and he drags me across the courtyard.

Spam is fleeing too, carrying an injured Java. But Ginger Ninja is nowhere to be seen.

We race into the forest. The tigers chase us, snarling, after our blood. The Shinto shrine comes into sight and we make a final mad dash between the bamboo stems. As the lead tiger pounces at us, we dive for the gateway ...

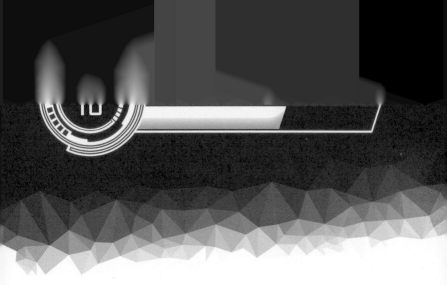

"Who the hell was *that*?" Java cries as she unplugs from her PlayPod. She limps over to me – her virtual injuries not faded yet. "The whole team almost got *killed* back there!"

"Take it easy, Java," Pac-Man says as he removes his hoody. "We all made it."

Java glares at him. "I was on 15%. I could've been fried!" Then she turns on me again. "So who was your buddy with the pulse-blades?"

"Shark," I groan as I sit up stiffly in my pod. My leg and arms throb from the after-effects of the pulse-blade cuts. "He's an enemy from the streets who followed me into VK."

Java throws up her hands. "Scott comes with baggage! First Ginger Ninja, now Shark. I knew he was a *risk* to the mission."

"Ginger Ninja helped us," Spam reminds her.

Java cocks her head. "Did he? Where was the ninja when we were fighting off ten tigers?"

Spam shrugs. I start to worry for Ginger Ninja, hoping he didn't burn out.

"He probably bolted," Pac-Man says.

"And I don't blame him," Spam adds.

Cookie is studying our battle in the temple on the console screen. "Scott, why didn't you use Trigger Time on Shark?"

"I did," I reply. "But he knows how to do it too."

"Well, it looks as if he's mastered it," Java says with a smirk. "He blazed you to shreds. Perhaps I should've recruited *him* instead of you!"

"That's unfair," Spam argues. "We got further today than we have in weeks."

"I agree," Pac-Man says. "We need to go back in."

"Not today." Pentium rolls into the room in his wheelchair. "You're all too drained. You'll risk Burn Out or, at the very least, memory loss. You need time back in the real world first."

"Scott should stay in the real world!" Java snaps. "He's no match for Shark and we don't need *shark bait* like him attracting any more danger to us."

She storms out of the room. Pentium follows her, trying to calm her down.

Spam raises his eyebrows at me but says nothing. Pac-Man gives me a friendly punch on the arm. "Don't worry about Java, Scott. She's often a bit cranky after VK. Me? I'm always starving. Let's go and grab some food."

He heads out the door; Spam goes with him. But I trail behind. I know Java is right. I'm no match for Shark and his pulse-blades – and that makes me a serious risk to the team.

I'm almost at the door when Cookie calls, "Scott! You should take a look at this."

The console monitor is replaying me being blazed by Shark. I'm powerless against his attacks. "Yeah, he's killing me," I sigh.

"No, look at the moment *after* he almost kills you."

Moving closer to the console, I watch as Pac-Man hurls the tiger at Shark then drags me away. I frown. "Am I missing something here?"

Cookie replays it again. "See this?" She points to Shark as the tiger attacks him and swipes off his dark shades. Shark kicks the tiger away then searches around for his shades like a blind man.

Cookie's lips curl into a sly smile. "His shades are a Mod, possibly to help boost Trigger Time. But he can't see without them."

"Any sign of your friend Shark?" Java asks in a bitter voice as we peer between the bamboo stems back in VK's virtual world. Pentium managed to persuade Java to let me back on the team but she still isn't happy about it.

I squint, shielding my eyes from the dazzling sun. The temple courtyard looks deserted. The tigers are back on their pedestals. "I don't see him—"

A *snap* behind makes us all turn and draw our weapons. I raise my fists, ready to fight. Then out of the forest scampers a small figure in a black outfit and mask.

"Not much of a ninja," Java sneers as she returns her sword to its sheath.

I grin. "Ginger Ninja, you're alive!"

"Where did you lot go?" complains my friend.

"We could say the same about you!" Pac-Man snorts.

Ginger Ninja shrugs. "He who fights and runs away lives to fight another day. But I came to warn you. Shark is still on the hunt."

"Where is he now?" I ask.

"He's searching the forest east of here."

"Good," Java says. "Then we approach from the west."

We keep a safe distance from the tigers as we skirt the courtyard and slip into the temple.

Inside, the air is cool. A wooden hall with high beams leads to an altar made of white marble. Shafts of golden sunlight send stripes across a flagstone floor. It makes me think of a chess board.

"There's the portal!" Spam says. He points to a rippling curtain behind the altar – its fabric is shimmering as if it were a butterfly's wings.

Spam heads towards it but Java plants a hand on his chest, stopping him in his tracks. "Something isn't right," Java says. "This looks too easy."

"Let me go first," Pac-Man volunteers. He takes a wary step onto the flagstone floor. Nothing happens. He moves forward another space ... waits ... then walks on.

"Perhaps the tigers are the only danger here?" Spam says as Pac-Man steps to his left.

Suddenly a spike shoots up from a tile into his foot. He screams as blood pours from his wound. Tugging his foot free, he staggers back before collapsing by the temple entrance.

"Guess I was wrong," Spam says with a grimace. He gives Pac-Man a health pack but it only heals his life-bar to 75%.

Java kneels down and bandages Pac-Man's foot. "At least we now know the danger."

"Yeah," I agree, "we just don't know which other tiles are booby-trapped!"

Ginger Ninja runs out of the temple, then returns a moment later with a length of bamboo. He hands it to me. "You can test each tile first."

I give him a look. "Some friend you are!"

But no one else is volunteering, so I step nervously onto the flagstone floor and re-trace Pac-Man's route. I jab the bamboo tip at each tile before moving on. All of a sudden, a spike appears and I jump back a square.

"That one was safe last time," Spam says.

"I know!" I reply as another spike drives up between my feet. I leap away before I'm skewered, turn and race back to my friends. But spikes are shooting up everywhere. It's as if I'm running in a forest of swords. I jump, skip and swerve. But on the last square a spike catches me in the leg. I dive for safety and land beside Pac-Man, alive but injured.

As Spam hunts for another health pack for me, Java studies the flagstone floor. "It must be totally random."

"Then how will we ever cross?" Pac-Man asks.

Spam is out of health packs, so I just lie back and grit my teeth against the pain. That's when I see the writing on the ceiling:

The more there is, the less you see.
Answer this and your guide I'll be.

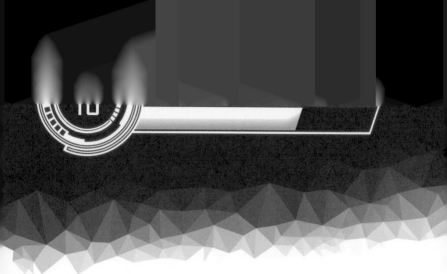

"Riddles! I hate riddles," Pac-Man complains as we stare at the words on the temple ceiling.

"Like 'em or hate 'em," Java says, "we need to come up with the answer if we're to cross this floor."

"Water?" I suggest as I clutch my bleeding leg.

She shakes her head. "That doesn't work."

"How about paint?" Ginger Ninja says.

Java frowns, thinking. "Could be, but you'd still see the paint."

Spam chews his lower lip.
"The more there is, the less—"
The sound of snarling
interrupts him.

"The smell of blood has woken the
tigers!" Ginger Ninja says, peering into the
courtyard. The stone statues leap off their
pedestals and prowl towards the temple.

Java helps Pac-Man to his feet. "Well, we
can't risk going on until we have the answer,"
she says. "Everyone, back to the shrine!"

Ginger Ninja offers me a hand up. Java
leads us out of the temple fast and back into
the forest. The stone tigers chase after us. We
push through the bamboo stems, trying to lose
them. But the gash in my leg is dripping blood
and leaving a trail for the tigers to follow.

Limping badly, I start to lag behind the
others. Ginger Ninja slows down to support

me. "Where now?" he asks as we near the Shinto shrine.

"Through the gateway," I reply. Ahead of us, Spam and Pac-Man dive in and vanish.

Ginger Ninja cocks an eyebrow. "A back door? Clever."

"Come on!" Java urges, and waves for us to hurry.

The tigers can sense their prey is close. They smash their way through the bamboo. I stagger on. We're almost at the shrine when I spot a girl far off in the forest. She's wearing shorts and a tight T-shirt, with a samurai sword strapped to her back. I recognise her in an instant.

"Where are you going?" Java cries as I dash off, leaving her and Ginger Ninja behind.

"*Kat-Ana?*" I shout. "Is that you?"

The faint sound of a song draws me deeper into the forest. I see a flick of dark hair ... then the gleam of a curved sword. I follow, forgetting my bleeding leg. Ahead, a shadow moves behind a thicket of bamboo. I pull apart the stems and come face-to-face with ... a stone tiger.

Its jaws open wide and the beast pounces. I try to fight it off but its claws tear into me. My life-bar drops: 73% ... 62% ... 51% ...

I kick the creature away but it bites into my leg: 45% ... 36% ...

Another tiger attacks me from behind. My vision becomes clouded with blood: 22% ... 13% ...

As I near the point of Burn Out, I see the flash of a blade and hear a girl's voice singing, "*London Bridge is falling down, falling down ...*"

"What the hell were you doing?" Java demands as my hoody comes off and I blink at the bright lights of the console room. "You almost burned out!"

"I-I-I saw ... Kat-Ana," I reply.

"Who?" Java barks.

I sit up in my PlayPod. My body feels as if it's been in a paper shredder. "Kate, my friend."

Spam frowns. "But you told me she died escaping VK?"

"Yes ... she burned out."

"Then perhaps you imagined her avatar," he suggests.

I shake my head. "No! She was singing her memory song and her face appeared in front of me just before I was unplugged."

"You're seeing things! Your brain's scrambled!" Java snaps. "VK must have overloaded it."

"Then how did Scott get to the back door?" Cookie asks from her console seat. "He was pinned down by tigers."

Java throws up her hands. "Oh, I don't know. Maybe Ginger Ninja saved him? The twerp disappeared again."

"Or else this Kat-Ana killed the tigers and carried Scott back to the shrine," Pac-Man suggests.

My heart lifts at the idea. But Java shoots it down: "Sorry, Scott, but if Kat-Ana's burned out, how could her avatar still be in the game?"

I don't have an answer. Then Pentium speaks up, "Your Kat-Ana could be a ghost in the machine."

I stare at him. "What are you saying?"

Pentium rolls forward and explains, "If your friend died half in and half out of VK, then her consciousness may have transferred into her avatar."

"That's ridiculous!" Java says. "Scott's chasing shadows. Now, our *only* focus is working out the riddle. I suggest we get some rest before trying again tomorrow."

We head to our dorm after a tense and silent dinner of rehydrated chilli and rice. As I throw a blanket over a bare mattress, I ask Pac-Man, "Why won't Java believe me about Kat-Ana?"

"Because she doesn't want to," he whispers back. "Java blames herself for her sister's death. She couldn't save her from Burn Out. So I guess the thought of her sister being trapped in the game is too much for Java to bear."

Pac-Man climbs into the top bunk. But I can't sleep. Thoughts of Kate swirl in my head. Could she be *alive* in the game? I know for a fact that her vital signs zeroed out. Yet I also saw an odd blue light in her eyes just as she died ...

In the opposite bunk to ours, Spam mutters to himself. "The more there is, the less you'll see. The more there is—"

"Will you shut up and turn off the light!"
Java moans, putting a pillow over her head.

Spam doesn't seem to hear, so I get up and
flick off the switch. All of a sudden, he bolts up
in his bed and declares, "I have the answer!"

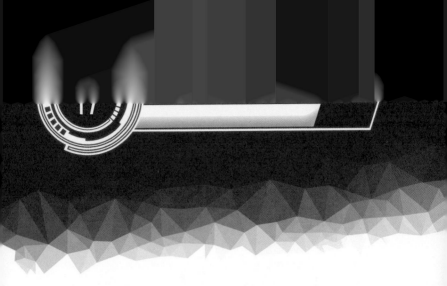

The next day, we're crouching at the entrance to the temple. I keep one eye on the stone tigers, the other on the forest. I'm meant to be on the lookout for Shark but really I'm hoping to spot Kat-Ana again. A patch of bamboo begins to rustle and shake ... but it turns out to be Ginger Ninja.

He scurries over. "What are you all waiting for?"

"Sunset," Java replies.

Ginger Ninja puts his head inside the gloomy temple. "But you won't be able to see a thing!"

"That's just it," Spam replies. "The more there is, the less you see. The answer to the riddle is *darkness*."

The sun dips below the horizon and the temple turns as black as a cave.

"Good luck crossing that death trap!" Ginger Ninja laughs. For a moment, nothing happens and I think Spam must have been wrong with his answer. Then a green glow is emitted from the flagstone floor. Different tiles light up – *a safe path over to the portal?*

"Well, who would have thought it?" Pac-Man says, and grins at his friend. "Spam has a working brain cell!"

We cross the floor fast, keeping to the glowing tiles and reach the rippling curtain of the portal unharmed.

"One more level to go!" Java says ...

The roar of the crowd is deafening as we appear in the centre of a huge combat arena. I look around in awe at the thousands of spectators watching from the stands. The fighting pit is splattered with the blood and body parts of countless defeated warriors. Thirty or more gladiators – armed with swords, shields and spears – surround us.

Cookie speaks via her comms link. "*The portal to the Last Level is beyond the Great Gate.*"

A massive wooden gateway with four locks around its iron ring handle stands at the far end of the pit. A diamond key is already in one lock. I spot three other keys – gold, silver and bronze – hanging at intervals around the arena.

"I'll get the gold key," Java says as she draws her sword. "Pac-Man and Spam, you go for the silver. Scott and Ginger Ninja, get the bronze. Go!"

We rush off in different directions. The gladiators split up after us.

I leap into the air, taking out a leather-clad warrior with a flying-kick. The next gladiator drives his spear at me. But I dodge to one side and smash my forearm onto the spear's shaft. It cracks in two and I chain-punch the fighter in the chest. He spits up blood and falls to the ground.

Ginger Ninja has little trouble taking out the other two gladiators in our path. In fact, they barely put up a fight against his whirlwind of kicks and punches.

Now, only one gladiator is left standing between us and the key. He's tall and dressed in black leather. For a moment, it looks like he's surrendering – he throws away his shield and drops his sword ... But after taking off his helmet, two pulse-blades burst into life from his knuckles.

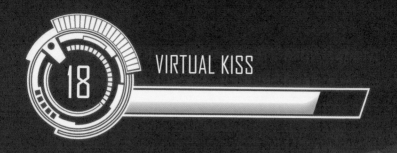

"Leave Shark to me," I tell Ginger Ninja. "You grab the key."

"That's fine by me," he replies, dashing away.

Ignoring Ginger Ninja, Shark bears down on me. "You're one slippery fish!" he growls. "But this time you *won't* get away."

He swipes at me with his pulse-blades, creating a blur of red laser. I focus on Trigger Time, slowing his attack just enough to avoid it. Then I leap into the air and counter with a

spinning hook-kick. My surprise move catches
Shark across the jaw and knocks off his shades.

Shark staggers
backwards and I see
panic in his exposed
white eyes. As he looks
around, as blind as a bat,

I kick him hard in the chest, sending him flying.
He lands in the blood-soaked dirt.

"Stay down, Shark," I order. "I'm not your
enemy. Vince Power is."

"What are you talking about?" he snarls.

"To play is to die," I explain. "VK causes
overload. If you lose your life-bar, you burn
out."

"*Really?*" Shark grins with his pointed
teeth. "Then let's play!"

He springs to his feet and pulls out a new pair of shades. Not the reaction I was hoping for.

Having lost my advantage, I'm forced to retreat as Shark launches a blistering blaze. I attempt Trigger Time but can't keep it up for long. Shark's pulse-blades become a deadly red blur and he burns my arm ... 82% ... Then cuts my leg ... 71% ... A slash to my thigh drops me to the ground ... 55% ...

Shark stands over me, his pulse-blades buzzing. "Time to burn out, Scott."

"No, time for *you* to burn out!" a gladiator in golden armour says.

Suddenly the tip of a samurai sword thrusts out of Shark's chest. He splutters blood and collapses to the ground, his life-bar on his chest blinking out.

I lie, open-mouthed and speechless, at the feet of my saviour. The gladiator removes a golden helmet to reveal a young girl's face – dark-eyed, pretty and with a nose-stud.

"Kate?" I gasp. "Is that *really* you?"

The gladiator nods. "Kat-Ana now," she replies, helping me to stand up. "But I promised I wouldn't forget you, Scott." She leans forward and kisses me. Feeling her lips upon mine, I can't believe that she's a ghost in the machine. Kate *has* to be real. *Alive!*

Kat-Ana sees the look in my eyes and reads my thoughts. "It's only a virtual kiss," she says with a sad smile.

"Hey, you two love birds!" Java shouts. "We need the bronze key ... NOW!" She points to a new wave of gladiators surging into the fighting pit.

Pac-Man and Spam already have the silver key. Java has the gold. But all three have paid a heavy price – they look battered, bloodied and broken. We hurry to join them. Ginger Ninja hands over the final key and Spam inserts it into the final lock.

"The gate won't open!" Pac-Man yells as he tugs on the iron ring at the centre of the gate.

We all pull together … but still the gate won't shift. The new gladiators are closing in, bristling with their swords and spears. We're outnumbered ten-to-one!

Java asks Cookie, "Where's the nearest back door?"

"*There isn't one on this level,*" she replies, her voice trembling.

"We're doomed!" Spam cries as he presses his back against the gate.

With nowhere to run and nowhere to hide, this will be a fight to the death. *Our* deaths. Burn Out guaranteed.

"*Remove the keys,*" Kat-Ana whispers to me.

I frown at her. It seems illogical. But I do as she says and start to pull out the keys from their locks.

"What do you think you're doing?!" Java shouts.

As I remove the last one, we hear a series of mechanical *clicks* and the gate swings open.

Grinning, I turn back to Kat-Ana ... but she's gone.

VK's Last Level is a world of polished jet-black marble. Lined with strips of neon-white light, it looks like a circuit board. Overhead, the sky rolls with dark thunder clouds, yet the level is as silent and cold as a tomb. The five of us stand alone. No other avatars are in sight.

"There's the terminal!" Java points to a computer console on an island of light in the distance. But between us and the terminal is a wide dark trench.

"*It's an Infinity Drop,*" Cookie says over the comms. "*Fall down there and you never hit bottom. Never die. Never escape the game.*"

"So how are we meant to cross it?" Pac-Man asks.

I peer into the abyss and judge the gap to be at least twenty metres. "The leap is impossible."

Pentium's voice sounds in our heads: "*Nothing is impossible in VK. Your mind can bend the rules of the game.*"

We all swap uneasy looks. No one is mad enough to try such a jump.

"OK, Wasp Boy," Java says as she hands me her last health pack. "You're the one with the death wish. You try first."

I stare at her, horrified. "You want me to *jump*?"

Java nods. "You're the risk-taker. If Trigger Time is possible, then a superman leap must be too."

I open my mouth to argue, then close it. Java's right. Besides, having got this far in VK, I realise there is no turning back now. It's do or die.

"Good luck," Ginger Ninja says as I back up as far as I can go.

The health pack heals my wounds and restores my life-bar to 100%. I'm as strong as I'll ever be. I imagine myself flying into the air, clearing the gap and leaping the Infinity Drop. With my mind focused, I sprint towards the edge and jump ...

I spring higher and further than gravity should allow. Below me is nothing but pitch-black darkness. Ahead of me is an island of light, rushing ever closer. Halfway across, I remember my leap in the Trial. How I missed the opposite roof and fell to my virtual death. The memory makes me lose focus. My jump starts to lose height. I begin to fall faster. The gap seems to widen ...

I hit the edge of the trench hard. My legs dangle over the Infinity Drop. My fingers claw at the island's smooth surface. I'm slipping and have to use all my strength to drag myself to safety.

"You did it!" Spam shouts, and punches the air.

"Yeah ... *just*," I gasp. I head over to the terminal, still trying to catch my breath. Cookie instructs me to type in a command and as soon as I press Enter, a light-bridge appears over the Infinity Drop. The others hurry across to join me.

"Awesome jump!" Pac-Man says. "You'll have—" His face turns to a grimace of pain. Then he falls to the floor, a knife in his back.

Before anyone can react, a throwing electro-star hits Spam in the neck. Sparks fly as the weapon stuns. Java goes for her sword but Ginger Ninja breaks her arm with a brutal side-kick.

"Ginger Ninja!" I cry. "What the hell are you doing?"

He turns to me and laughs. "I'm *not* Ginger Ninja." Before my eyes, he transforms from a small black-suited figure in a ninja mask into a tall, handsome man with a mane of silver-grey hair.

My legs go weak at the shock of what I'm seeing. "Vince Power!" I gasp.

Vince flashes a toothy grin. "The one and only."

"What have you done to Ginger Ninja?" I demand.

Vince gives me a look of pity. "Oh, I'm afraid your friend Ginger Ninja burned out a while back. But his avatar still had its use. I could fool you with it and make you trust me."

For a moment, I can't grasp the truth. "But if you're *really* Vince ... why have you been helping us?"

"VK's a game, Scott," he replies with a grin. "I wanted to see how far you'd get. To be honest, I never expected you to reach the Last Level." The smile drops from his face. "But this is where the game ends for you."

Vince Power strides towards me. "Did you really think my Analysts wouldn't spot four rogue gamers? The only thing I didn't know was how you were hacking in and out of VK. Back doors – very clever! But they won't save you now."

His eyes spark blue and his hands crackle with electricity. Bolts of lightning arc from his fingertips and strike me down before I can defend myself. My body twists in pain and I'm flung back to the edge of the Infinity Drop.

"It's a *long* way down," Vince says with glee. "And there's no back door!"

Powerless to stop him, I can only stare in terror at the drop below. Then out of nowhere Java charges at Vince, her Amazonian avatar driving him to the very edge of the Infinity Drop.

"NO!" I cry as they *both* tumble over.

My focus on them is so intense, I enter Trigger Time. I watch as Vince slowly falls backwards. Streaks of lightning snaking in the air. His scream sounding like a long low moan. Java toppling after him. Her sword spinning away into darkness …

But now I'm free of Vince's lightning grip, I can move again and my reactions are ultra-fast compared to the others. As Java tumbles forward, I make a grab for her trailing leg …

With Trigger Time over, VK returns to normal speed. Vince's scream rises to a high shriek as his avatar plunges into the Infinity Drop and disappears.

Java dangles like a leaf in the wind. I tighten my grip on her foot. With my avatar's super strength, I pull her back onto the island. We lie side by side, panting and trembling.

"And you call me a risk-taker!" I gasp at Java.

She laughs, despite the pain she must be in. "You can't have *all* the glory, Wasp Boy."

Spam sits up weakly and tugs the electro-star from his neck. "W-What … happened?"

"Don't worry," I reply with a grin. "Vince Power just dropped by."

Pac-Man groans. He's bleeding badly but still alive. While Java tends to his wound and straps up her own arm, I head over to the terminal.

There's just a screen and a keyboard. "What do I need to do, Cookie?"

"*I'll stream the virus to your avatar,*" she replies.

My fingers fly across the keyboard as I automatically input the complex code. After a few minutes of furious typing, a red icon flashes up on the screen.

"*As soon as you press the Execute command, VK will corrupt and collapse,*" Cookie explains. "*You'll need to reach a back door fast.*"

I turn to Java, who is helping Pac-Man across the light-bridge along with Spam. Once they're at the white-gated portal to the previous level, Java nods to me. My finger hovers above the red Execute icon.

"What are you waiting for?" Java asks.

The fate of VK is in my hands. It's what we've fought so hard for. But I can't bring myself to press the icon. To end VK would be to end …

Kat-Ana appears at my side. "Do it," she says.

I look at her with tears in my eyes. "But you'll die."

"I'm already dead," Kat-Ana replies softly. She places a hand on my heart. "But I'll live on in here."

She presses Execute.

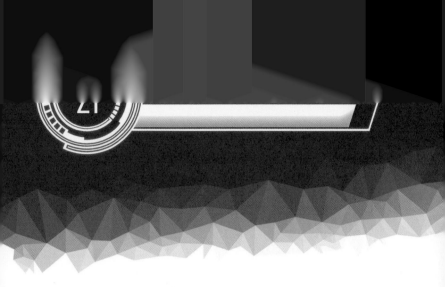

21

Thunder rumbles in the clouds above and the neon strip lights explode like fireworks. The jet-black marble ground cracks and crumbles as an earthquake shakes the Last Level to its core.

I race across the light-bridge to the portal. The others dive in. I take one last look at Kat-Ana – she's ringed in a halo of light on the island. Then I jump into the portal myself.

The gladiator pit is caving in too. As the arena collapses like a deck of cards, spectators crash into oblivion. Rifts open up in the sandy pit, swallowing gladiators whole.

"We have to get to the back door on the previous level," Java says.

The portal back to the temple shimmers on the far side of the pit. We dash past the chaos, dodging warriors and leaping over holes in the ground. Pac-Man stumbles and falls, weak from losing so much blood. I take hold of his arm to help Java to carry him. But a gladiator steps into our path. He swings an axe at our heads.

"Sorry, no time to chat," Spam says, and then blasts the gladiator aside with his laser rifle.

We reach the portal and jump back into the Temple of the Ten Tigers. Dawn has just broken and a blood-red sun is peeking above the horizon. Its first rays enter the temple.

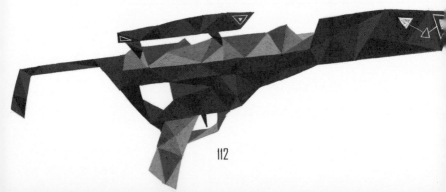

"Hurry!" Spam urges as the glowing tiles across the flagstone floor begin to fade.

We follow the safe path. But the sun's rays strike the floor before we're all the way across. Spikes shoot up, forcing us to dive for the entrance – we make it, just. Then the temple begins to shudder and its beams start to split. Roof tiles rain down as we scramble to our feet.

Cookie's voice shouts in our heads: "*VK is corrupting fast ... risk of losing wireless connection ... get out now—*"

Her signal is cut off by static. We make for the Shinto shrine but the courtyard lurches like a ship in a storm as the virus spreads. The stone tigers crumble to dust. The forest ahead flickers and the bamboo turns from barbed wire into razor-sharp grass and back to bamboo. We fight our way through the deadly changing forest. Barbed wire rips at our skin.

Grass blades cut our legs. Bamboo blocks our path.

By some miracle, we reach the shrine alive and throw ourselves at the gateway ... only to land on the paving on the other side.

"Why's the back door not working?" Spam asks, his voice high with panic.

My stomach twists into a knot as I realise, "Vince Power must have disabled it!"

"What about the well?" Java says. "Ginger Ninja wasn't with us back then, so Vince can't know about that one."

We race out of the forest, heading back to the Wild West town. The landscape is now so corrupted by the virus that the ground falls away behind us. The end of the virtual world is snapping at our heels.

At the crossroads of the Wild West town we find the well. But the virus has already changed it into a solid block of granite.

"What now?" Spam cries. "We're trapped!"

"No. The waterfall!" I say. "It's our last hope."

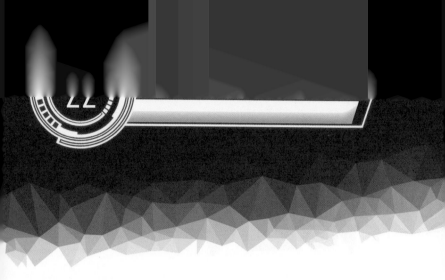

22

Beneath the Reaper's mountain, an eruption rumbles like a giant waking from a long sleep. The cave shudders and the lava pool boils over, sending a river of molten rock flowing after us as we stagger along the tunnel. Pac-Man's life-bar is critical – 9% – and he can hardly stand upright. Half-carrying him, we burst out of the cave. The waterfall still pours down the mountainside, but as we get nearer, the crashing water begins to slow.

"Go! Go! GO!" Java shouts. We dash towards the waterfall in a race for our lives. The roaring torrent of water shrinks ... to a steady flow ... to a feeble shower ...

Spam jumps in first, followed by Pac-Man, then Java. I leap in as the last trickle of water falls ...

॥

"Did he make it?"

"I don't know. The console lost its wireless connection at the last second."

"He's breathing!"

"That means nothing if his mind is gone."

The voices sound far off. Like a distorted radio. Streams of zeros and ones pass before my eyes. Then the world blinks into life, as if I've been plugged into a power socket, and Cookie's face appears before me.

She smiles brightly. "Welcome back to the real world, Scott."

Java and Spam help me from my PlayPod. My body is stiff and weak. My mind feels scrambled. But my spirits lift as soon as I see Pac-Man alive and well. He gives me a thumbs-up from his PlayPod, then tucks into an energy bar.

"Congratulations," Pentium says as he wheels over in his chair. "VK is offline. For good."

Spam high-fives me and I grin at our success. We did it! We *actually* did it. Then the smile drops from my face. "What about all the gamers?" I ask as Cookie passes me a recovery drink. "Are they dead?"

Cookie shakes her head. "They may be a bit confused and disorientated. But the failsafe would've disconnected them. You, on the other hand, had a hacked-in wireless connection. If that had broken, there'd have been no coming back."

"A millisecond longer and you'd have been brain-dead!" Spam laughs.

"Not much change there then," Java teases me. She hands me an energy bar.

I laugh too. "Next time you're hanging over an Infinity Drop, Java, remind me to let you go!" I knock back the drink, take a bite of the bar and instantly feel better. "What about Vince?" I ask.

Pentium sighs. "There's no escape from the Infinity Drop. Plus, he would have still been falling when the virus struck. He's either dead, or he might as well be, with his mind severed from his body."

"So it's over?"

Pentium nods. "People are no longer slaves to VK."

My heart lifts with joy and relief. VK is down. The Elite Gamers are free. Kate's death is avenged. Vince Power is no more. Yet our victory feels bittersweet now I know that Kat-Ana is gone for ever.

I put down my drink. "But what happens now?" I ask.

"The world has a chance to re-boot," Pentium says. He leans forward, looks me in the eye and smiles. "The question is, what will *you* do with your life?"